# MAGNETIC SLIME

BY
LOUISE NELSON

Published in 2022 by Windmill Books,
an Imprint of Rosen Publishing
29 East 21st Street, New York, NY 10010

© 2022 Booklife Publishing
This edition is published by arrangement with Booklife Publishing

All rights reserved. No part of this book may be reproduced in any form without permission in writing from the publisher, except by a reviewer.

Edited by: Madeline Tyler
Illustrated by: Danielle Rippengill

Cataloging-in-Publication Data

Names: Nelson, Louise.
Title: Magnetic slime / Louise Nelson.
Description: New York : Windmill, 2022. | Series: Slimy science | Includes glossary and index.
Identifiers: ISBN 9781499489576 (pbk.) | ISBN 9781499489590 (library bound) | ISBN 9781499489583 (6pack) | ISBN 9781499489606 (ebook)
Subjects: LCSH: Gums and resins, Synthetic--Juvenile literature. | Magnetic materials--Juvenile literature. | Handicraft--Juvenile literature.
Classification: LCC TP978.N45 2022 | DDC 620.1'924--dc23

Printed in the United States of America

CPSIA Compliance Information: Batch CWWM22: For Further Information contact Rosen Publishing, New York, New York at 1-800-237-9932

## SAFETY AND RESPONSIBILITY INFO FOR GROWN-UPS

Any ingredients used could cause irritation, so don't play with slime for too long, don't put it near your face, and keep it away from babies and young children.

Always wash your hands before and after making slime. Choose kid-safe glues and non-toxic ingredients, and always make sure there is an adult present.

Don't substitute ingredients—we cannot guarantee the results.

Leftover slime can be stored for one more use for up to a week in a sealed container and out of the reach of children. For hygiene reasons, we do not recommend storing slime that has been used in a classroom environment.

Slime is not safe for pets.

Wear a mask around powdered ingredients and goggles around liquid ingredients. Before throwing your slime away, cut it into lots of small pieces. Don't put slime down the drain—always put it in the trash.

MAGNETIC SLIME!

**IMAGE CREDITS:** All images are courtesy of Shutterstock.com, unless otherwise specified. With thanks to Getty Images, Thinkstock Photo and iStockphoto. Cover – Zhe Vasylieva, balabolka, Dado Photos, xnova, Lithiumphoto, New Africa, fullempty, Pixfiction. Images used on every page: Heading Font – Zhe Vasylieva. Background – Lithiumphoto. Grid – xnova. Splats – Sonechko57. 2 – Purple Clouds. 4 – jarabee123. 5 – Natallia Boroda, Purple Clouds. 6 – Agnieszka Baca. 7 – New Africa. 8 – Kuzina Natali, New Africa, Stenko Vlad. 10 – redknapper, tkyszk, Pixfiction. 11 – anmbph, Martin Charles, Liudmila Savushkina, chupong cuppanimitkul. 12&13 – Kuzina Natali, Mona Makela. 14 – jarabee123. 15 – Fototocam. 17&18 – New Africa, Purple Clouds. 19 – fullempty. 20 – Pixel-Shot. 21 – New Africa, Purple Clouds, Kenishirotie. 22&23 – Purple Clouds, Stratos Gianniko.

# CONTENTS

PAGE 4 — IT'S SLIME TIME!
PAGE 6 — THE SCIENCE OF SLIME
PAGE 8 — THE OBSERVATION STATION
PAGE 9 — SAFETY FIRST!
PAGE 10 — STUCK ON YOU
PAGE 12 — GET STUCK IN
PAGE 14 — TIME FOR SLIME
PAGE 16 — LET'S EXPERIMENT
PAGE 20 — THE OBSERVATIONS
PAGE 22 — QUESTION TIME
PAGE 24 — GLOSSARY AND INDEX

Words that look like this can be found in the glossary on page 24.

# IT'S SLIME TIME!

It's sticky, gooey, yucky fun. Hands up if you love slime! Slime is bouncy, stretchy, and oozy. But what is slime really?

!! NERD ALERT !!
Slime is a non-Newtonian fluid. This means that it doesn't act like other <u>liquids</u>, such as water or milk.

Everything you can see is made of some kind of stuff. Wood, paper, glass, metal, and all other types of "stuff" are called materials. Slime is a material that has the following **properties**:

NOT QUITE SOLID

SQUEEZY

FLOWS BUT NOT RUNNY

NOT QUITE LIQUID

STRETCHY

# THE SCIENCE OF SLIME

Many animals make their own natural slime. When opossums are afraid, they play dead, foam at the mouth, and make a stinky green slime from their bottoms! This scares away any **predators**.

!! NERD ALERT !!
Did you know you make your own slime inside your body every day?! It is snot!

# WE CAN ALSO MAKE SLIME WITH SCIENCE!

Never touch chemicals without an adult!

When we mix two chemicals together, it can change their properties. By mixing the correct chemicals together, we can turn liquids, powders, and other things into slime!

# THE OBSERVATION STATION

Are you feeling scientific? Let's see what we can observe about slime . . .

**!! NERD ALERT !!**
Observing something means you watch it and pay attention to what it does. You could take photos or write your observations in a notebook.

CAN I BLOW A BUBBLE WITH A STRAW?

HOW HARD CAN I SQUEEZE IT?

HOW FAR CAN I STRETCH IT?

# SAFETY FIRST!

## THE GOLDEN RULES

1. Always make slime with a grown-up.

2. Don't swap in other ingredients because different **reactions** could happen.

3. DON'T EAT SLIME, and keep it away from your face.

!! NERD ALERT !!
If you are **sensitive** to any ingredients, wear long sleeves and gloves or use a different recipe.

# STUCK ON YOU

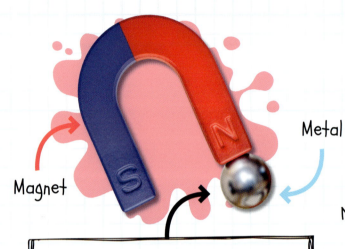

Magnet — Metal

A magnet is an object that **attracts** some metals.

A magnet has two **poles**, north and south.

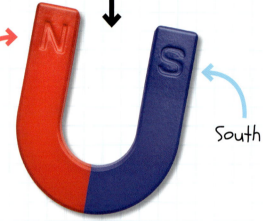

North — South

The same ends push each other away.

North —  South

Two different ends pull toward each other.

# MAGNETS ARE ATTRACTED TO:

STEEL CUTLERY

IRON NAILS

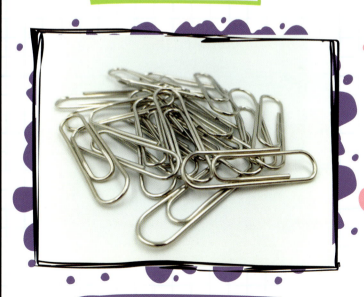

STEEL PAPER CLIPS

STEEL KEYS

# GET STUCK IN

## TO MAKE MAGNETIC SLIME, YOU WILL NEED:

- ☐ 1/4 cup (60 ml) of white or clear school glue (PVA)
- ☐ 2 tablespoons of liquid starch
- ☐ 2 tablespoons of iron oxide powder
- ☐ Safety First!

### DON'T FORGET!
Always make slime with a responsible adult!

(Your grown-up can buy this online!)

Adults should open and mix in the iron oxide powder.

You should also wear a mask. You do NOT want any dust from this near your face!

## METHOD:

1. Mix the glue with the iron oxide powder.

2. Pour the liquid starch in.

3. As soon as you add the starch, the chemical reaction will begin. Start stirring and watch what happens!

4. Mix and knead until your slime feels slimy!

If your slime is too sticky, add a tiny bit more starch. If it is too stringy, add a tiny bit more glue.

13

# TIME FOR SLIME

When you play with magnetic slime, it will feel just like regular slime.

IT WILL STRETCH ...

... AND IT WILL OOZE ...

... AND IT WILL SQUISH!

But when you add a magnet, things get interesting!

You will need a strong magnet to play with your slime. Your grown-up may need to buy this online. It needs to be strong so that the iron powder can feel its pull through the sticky slime.

## MAGNETS COME IN LOTS OF SHAPES AND SIZES!

HORSESHOES

ROUND

SPHERES

BARS

# LET'S EXPERIMENT

## YOU WILL NEED:

☐ Magnetic slime

☐ A magnet

## THE QUESTION:

Will the slime move toward the magnet?

## THE TEST:

We will put the magnet close to the slime to see if the slime is attracted to the magnet.

## THE EXPERIMENT:

Hold your magnet close to your slime and observe what happens.

You could do this experiment in lots of different ways. What else could you change?

## THE RESULTS:

When you are holding your magnet close enough to the slime, the slime should be attracted to the magnet!

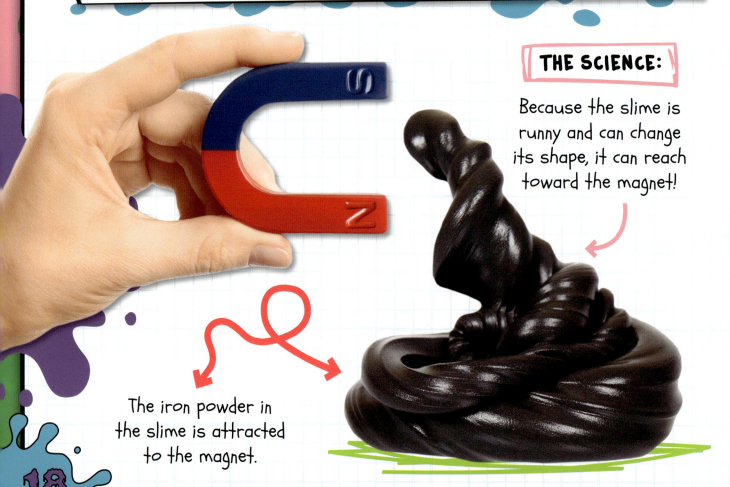

### THE SCIENCE:

Because the slime is runny and can change its shape, it can reach toward the magnet!

The iron powder in the slime is attracted to the magnet.

## EXPERIMENT ONE:

What happens when the slime is hanging down?

## EXPERIMENT TWO:

What directions can the magnet make your slime move in?

!! NERD ALERT !!
Write down everything you notice, or take pictures and videos. It's important for scientists to record what they find.

# THE OBSERVATIONS

When scientists do an experiment, the things they notice are called observations. Try writing down all the things you notice when playing with magnets and slime.

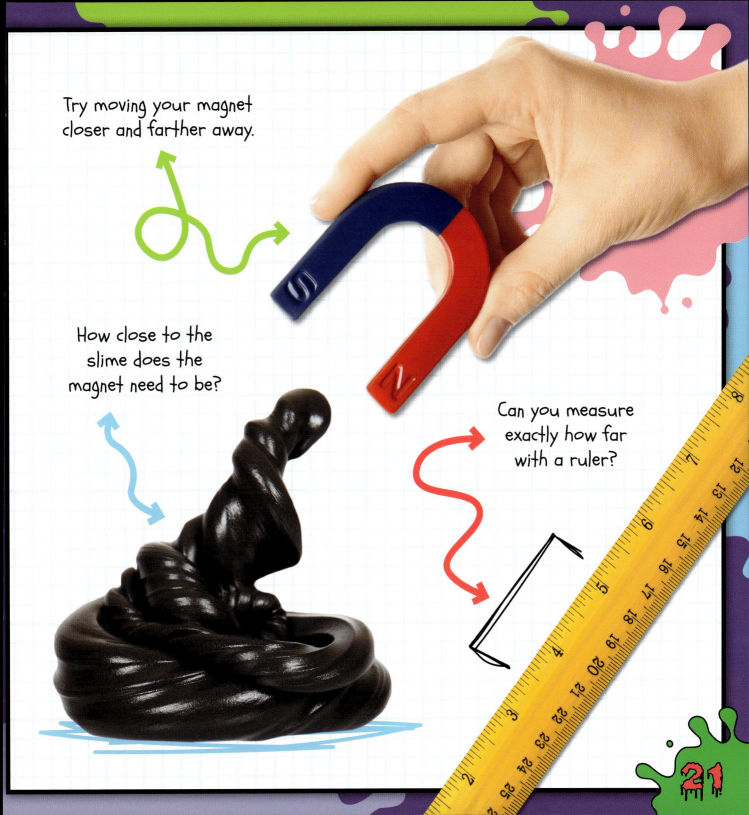

# QUESTION TIME

What other experiments can you do with your magnetic slime? Don't forget to take photos, make notes, and draw pictures of your slime experiments!

**NOTES:**

**EXPERIMENT ONE:**

**EXPERIMENT TWO:**

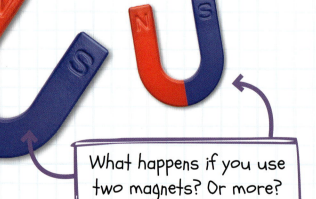

Does it bounce?

What happens if you use two magnets? Or more?

# GLOSSARY

**ATTRACTS** pulls toward

**CHEMICALS** matter that can cause changes to other matter when mixed

**LIQUIDS** materials that flow, such as water

**POLES** the farthest ends of a thing

**PREDATORS** animals that hunt other animals for food

**PROPERTIES** features of something

**REACTIONS** changes that happen when two or more things come into contact with each other

**SENSITIVE** reacts strongly to something

**SOLID** firm and stable, not a liquid

**SPHERES** shapes that are round and solid

# INDEX

**CHEMICALS** 7
**IRON** 11, 12, 13, 15, 18
**LIQUIDS** 4, 5, 7, 12, 13
**MATERIALS** 5
**OBSERVATIONS** 8, 17, 20–21
**OPOSSUMS** 6
**PROPERTIES** 5, 7
**RULERS** 21
**SOLIDS** 5
**STRETCHING** 4, 5, 8, 14, 23